Sleepover

by Miriam Sklar

ISBN: 978-1-338-75082-9
Illustrated by John Lund

Published by Scholastic Inc., 557 Broadway, New York, NY 10012

10 9 8 7 6 5 4 68 25 26 27/0

Printed in Jiaxing, China. First printing, January 2021.

Pack my PJs.

Pack my robe.

Pack my slippers.

Pack my toothbrush.

Pack my book.

Pack my bear.

Pack my snack!